ONCE UPON A GOAT

DAN RICHARDS
PICTURES BY ERIC BARCLAY

ALFRED A. KNOPF

New York

Once upon a time,
in a faraway kingdom,
a king and queen
wished for a child.

"Yes, but where would we put it?" asked the king.

"Next to the vase on the hearth, naturally," replied the queen.

"Or beside the roses in the garden," the king added.

"Oh, yes. Perfect," agreed the queen.

One day, their fairy godmother stopped by for a visit.

"Tell me what you desire," she asked.
"We'd like to start a family," said the king.
"We're not particular," said the queen. "Glowing skin, bright eyes, and hair like ocean waves should do."

"Hmm . . . ," said their fairy godmother.

"A boy would be great," added the king. "But any kid will do."

"Of course," answered their fairy godmother. "Look on your doorstep when the moon is full."

At the next full moon, the king and queen ran to the door.
"Let it be a boy," said the king.
"With hair like ocean waves," said the queen.

"Baah," said the goat.

"I wanted a baby," cried the queen.

"It's my fault," wailed the king. "I said any kid would do.
But I never meant—*this*."

Reluctantly, the king
and queen brought the
little beast into their home.

"Look on the bright side," said the king. "We can still hold it like a baby."

"It has a goatee," replied the queen.

"We won't need to change its diapers," said the queen.

"That's disgusting," replied the king.

"At least it loves the royal roses," said the king.
"That's it. It has to go," commanded the queen.

"I guess we're better off now,"
said the queen sadly.
"A stand had to be taken.
For the roses," replied the king.
"Of course," said the queen.

That night it rained. Hard.

"It's not our fault we were given a goat," said the queen.

"Not our fault at all," added the king. "And yet I wonder if we were right to send the little fellow away on such a blustery night."

"Clearly he lacks the good sense to find shelter.
I suppose he could come in just for a bit to dry off."

"He looks hungry," said the king. "Maybe he could share a nibble or two from our meal."

"It's late. We can hardly send him away now," said the queen. "He shall have to stay in our room for the night."

"It's only for the night," said the king.

One night turned into weeks, and weeks into months.

Before long, their fairy godmother
returned for a visit. "How is everything?"

"Wonderful," replied the king and queen.
"Perfect. May I see the child?"

"Isn't he darling?" said the king.
"A blessing," added the queen.

"You must be joking," said their fairy godmother. "It's a goat."

"Yes, left on the doorstep when the moon was full, just like you said."

"Uh-oh," said their fairy godmother. "I'll be back."

"Oh, dear."

"This is for the best. Really."

"My sincere apologies for the misunderstanding. I'll just return the goat, and that will be that."

"Wait," said the queen.

"Perhaps there is an alternative," said the king at last.

"Yes, I see your point," said their fairy godmother.